The Stowaway Mouse

The Stowaway Mouse

by Daisy Nell

Illustrations by George Ulrich

ISBN # 978-0-615-45507-5

Text set in Hoefler font.
Book design by Judy Arisman, www.arismandesign.com
Illustrations by George Ulrich, www.georgeulrich.com

The Schooner *Ardelle*, as depicted in *The Stowaway Mouse*, is a real schooner, built in Essex, MA. In reality her builder, captain, and owner is Harold Burnham, www.burnhamboatbuilding.com. The captain in the story is not intended to represent the actual captain.

Published by Penrose Press, Essex, MA, 01929.
www.daisynell.com.

Printed and bound in Canada

This book is dedicated to the children of the Essex Elementary School's 2nd grade of 2011, whose names are listed at the back of this book.

Geroge Ulrich would like to dedicate his drawings in this book to his favorite twins, Thing 1 and Thing 2, Jack and Libby, with love from Grampy.

The story, *The Stowaway Mouse*, uses some expressions that might be unfamiliar:

A *stowaway* is a person, or even a mouse, who sneaks on board a ship without permission.

A *"Mickey"* is what some people informally call a mouse, just like sometimes we call a turkey a "Tom."

The term, *"ready about"* is a command that sailors use to warn others in the crew that the boat is about to change directions. If other crew members aren't ready for this change, they could be hit by the flapping of ropes and slapping of sails that happen until the wind fills the sails again in the other direction.

Acknowledgements

The Stowaway Mouse is the result of a folk music and songwriting project in the second grade of the elementary school in Essex, Massachusetts. Two classes of inspiring children worked with me to learn about traditional folk music and instruments and to create songs based on local history. As the *Ardelle* took shape at the edge of the Essex River, *The Stowaway Mouse* also took shape, first as a song, then a book. Thank you to the Massachusetts Cultural Council and the PTO for the grants that funded this school residency, to music teacher Richard Carpenter and librarian Susan Hardy for coordinating the grants, and to second grade teachers Jeannine Stanley and Andrew Burnett.

In the making of this book, I would like to express boundless appreciation to George Ulrich for his inspired illustrations and his generosity of spirit, patience, and expertise. It was pure serendipity to have connected with him, thanks to Steve Willard and our dear, late friend, Steve Wainwright. In addition, my heartfelt thanks go to Judy Arisman, of Arisman Design Studio, for her creative work in designing this book and her assistance in making the idea of this book into a reality. I am also grateful to other members of *The Stowaway Mouse* "crew" for their help with this project: Linda Amero, photo editor; Martha Bustin, text editor; and Lauren Means, proofreader. In the making of the CD, Eric Kilburn of Wellspring Sound was a tremendous resource, friend, and sound engineer.

(continued)

Special thanks to Harold Burnham for maintaining the traditions of shipbuilding in Essex; to Laurie Fullerton and Harold's family; to the building crew of the *Ardelle*.

Finally, I would like to thank my family, my grandchildren Hunton and Cecelia Russell for their invaluable editorial comments, and, most of all, my beloved husband Stan Collinson, for his steadfast support, encouragement, humor, advice, and musicality.

The
Stowaway
Mouse

There were people gathered all around
To see the new schooner in this old town,
Down by the river, ready to go
Out to the bay where the oceans do flow.
There was a little mouse, but people
     couldn't see him.
He lived inside of the Essex museum.
He never went farther than he dared—
He was a little mouse, and he was scared.

So many had come to see the new boat,

To see her splash and see her float.

Built brand new and named *Ardelle*,

The sights she'd see no one could tell—

Wind and whales and waves that splash,

Sun and rain and lightning flash.

The mouse took a breath, and—1-2-3—

He scampered up the frame and off

    to sea.

Oh no, what are you going to do?

Now that you've become a member of the crew.

Oh no, where are you going to go?

Heading off to sea where the big winds blow.

No one saw him; he was on board,

He scurried down below where the food
   was stored.

He found a pair of the captain's shoes

And crawled right in for a little snooze.

He woke up feeling a stream of air

Blowing through the boat right through
   his hair.

He ran and hid in the coffee pot,

And there was the captain tying up a
   knot.

The boat was rocking back and forth,

Heading out to sea east by north.

The mouse was hungry, but he was afraid.

He saw a crate of apples that he could raid.

He took a little bite, and it went crunch,

And that was the end of the mouse's
     lunch.

The captain hollered, and he did yell,

"Mates, we've got a Mickey on the
     Schooner *Ardelle!*"

Oh no, what are you going to do?

Now that you've become a member of the crew.

Oh no, where are you going to go?

Heading off to sea where the big winds blow.

Well, the mouse he did skedaddle up
    to the deck
And tried to get a grip without breaking
    his neck.
Just when the mouse was feeling fine,
Along came the captain and his crew
    of nine—
Yo heave ho and raise the sails—
Climbing up the rigging to look for whales.
The captain said, as he gazed upon the
    sea,
"Better find Molly and bring her to me."

The captain stood behind the wheel.

The mouse was in a hole near the captain's

　heel.

"Oh, here comes Molly," the crew did

　cheer,

But no new person did appear.

The mouse looked out. He took a chance.

Then ran like crazy up the captain's pants.

For there was Molly, tall and mean,

The biggest old cat he'd ever seen!

Oh no, what are you going to do?

Now that you've become a member of the crew.

Oh no, where are you going to go?

Heading off to sea where the big winds blow.

The little mouse ran. He did his best.

He hid in the pocket of the captain's vest.

Underneath his hat he then did sneak.

He didn't really dare, but he had to peek.

He saw then what the sailors knew.

The captain kept a mouse catcher on
  the crew.

The captain shouted like a thunder crack,

"Ready about, we're turning back!"

The captain said then in a voice so low,

"Hey, little mousey back home you go.

You see, this voyage was our practice run,

But I'll have to send you packing when

    the day is done.

You would never get away from my old cat

And I can't keep you under my hat.

But now you have a story, forever to tell:

For a day you were crew on the Schooner

    Ardelle!"

Oh no, what are you going to do?

Now that you've become a member of the crew.

Oh no, where are you going to go?

Heading off to sea where the big winds blow.

The Story Behind the Story

In addition to the people who call Essex, Massachusetts, their home-town, others might come to Essex to have a fried clam dinner, shop for antiques, or maybe just take a scenic drive along the river. Today, few among these residents or visitors think of Essex as, at heart, a shipbuilding town. Yet Essex has seen over 4000 boats built over the course of its history.

Happily, this shipbuilding tradition continues right up to our present times. In 2011, Harold Burnham, whose family has been building boats in this town for over 300 years, built a schooner named *Ardelle*. The day it was finally finished and launched was a major event in Essex, just as it has always been. No matter how carefully the boat has been built and prepared, people feel excitement and curiosity until the new ship is safely floating. It was a great day in Essex when *Ardelle* first entered the water and sailed. Harold Burnham, who is also the *Ardelle*'s captain, named this boat after his grandmother. If you named a boat for your grandmother, what would the name be?

So, what is a schooner? A schooner is a sturdy wooden ship with (usually) two masts to hold the sails. These boats were built strong, to be able to go out fishing in the rough waters off the New England coast, and then be able to sail swiftly home with the fish they caught. A schooner is the symbol of the nearby city of Gloucester, the old-est fishing port in the country. Many of the schooners that sailed from Gloucester were built in Essex. Gradually schooners were replaced by boats with engines, which did not rely on the wind. Over the past fifty years, the last working fishing schooners have all but gone away. In Gloucester, however, you can still see schooners, including the *Ardelle*, that take people out for a few hours each day. The captain and the mates are the real crew, but passengers can help the crew perform certain tasks. They might help raise the sails and sing the old "Heave Ho" work songs, called sea chanteys.

The *Ardelle* is a type of schooner known as a "pinky," which means that both of its ends are pointed. Sometimes, from a distance, you can't tell whether she is coming or going! Why are boats often referred to as "she"? Sailors trust that, if they take care of their boats, their boats will take care of them, like a good mother, and will bring them safely home.

What happens when a "Mickey" stows away on the Schooner *Ardelle* on her very first voyage? Here's what I wrote with the second grade in Essex, Massachusetts. I hope you like the story and the song included with this book.

—*Daisy Nell*

ESSEX ELEMENTARY SCHOOL 2ND GRADE, 2011

Ms. Stanley's class:

Heather Adams
Dylan Burbridge
Ryan Crompton
Eve DiZio
Bonnie Gerhardt
Tyler Huber
Samuel Kenney
William Kenney
Amelia Laino
Madison Lawler
Amelia Lee
Eden Mayer
Connor McGrath
Sean O'Neill
Aidan Parker
Sean Phelan
Olivia Renzi
Elizabeth Rizotti
Noah Stevens
Oliver Tolo
Eliza Woodward
Matthew Yakabowskas

Mr. Burnett's class:

Jack Ashley
Faith Burroughs
Faith Costello
Samuel Foss
Emily Fossa
Dylan Gregory
Keven Harding
Griffen Kempskie
Nicole LaPointe
Eden MacDonald
Paige Marshall
James Owen McKenna
Cooper O'Brien
Phillip Parker
Morgan Phippen
Jack Roberts
Braden Sheahan
Nora Smith
Jonah Tomaiolo
Trenten Whittemore
Anna Whitten